For my two wee stars, Alice and Archie – S.H.

For Sophie and Alex – S.M.

EGMONT
We bring stories to life

First published in Great Britain 2018 by Egmont UK Limited
The Yellow Building, 1 Nicholas Road, London W11 4AN

www.egmont.co.uk

Text copyright © Sam Hay 2018
Illustrations copyright © Sarah Massini 2018

The moral rights of the author and illustrator have been asserted.

ISBN 978 1 4052 8430 1

# STAR IN THE JAR

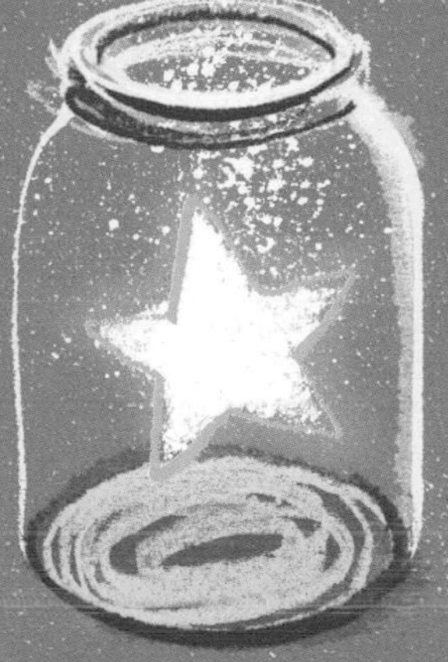

SAM HAY

SARAH MASSINI

EGMONT

My little brother likes looking for treasure.

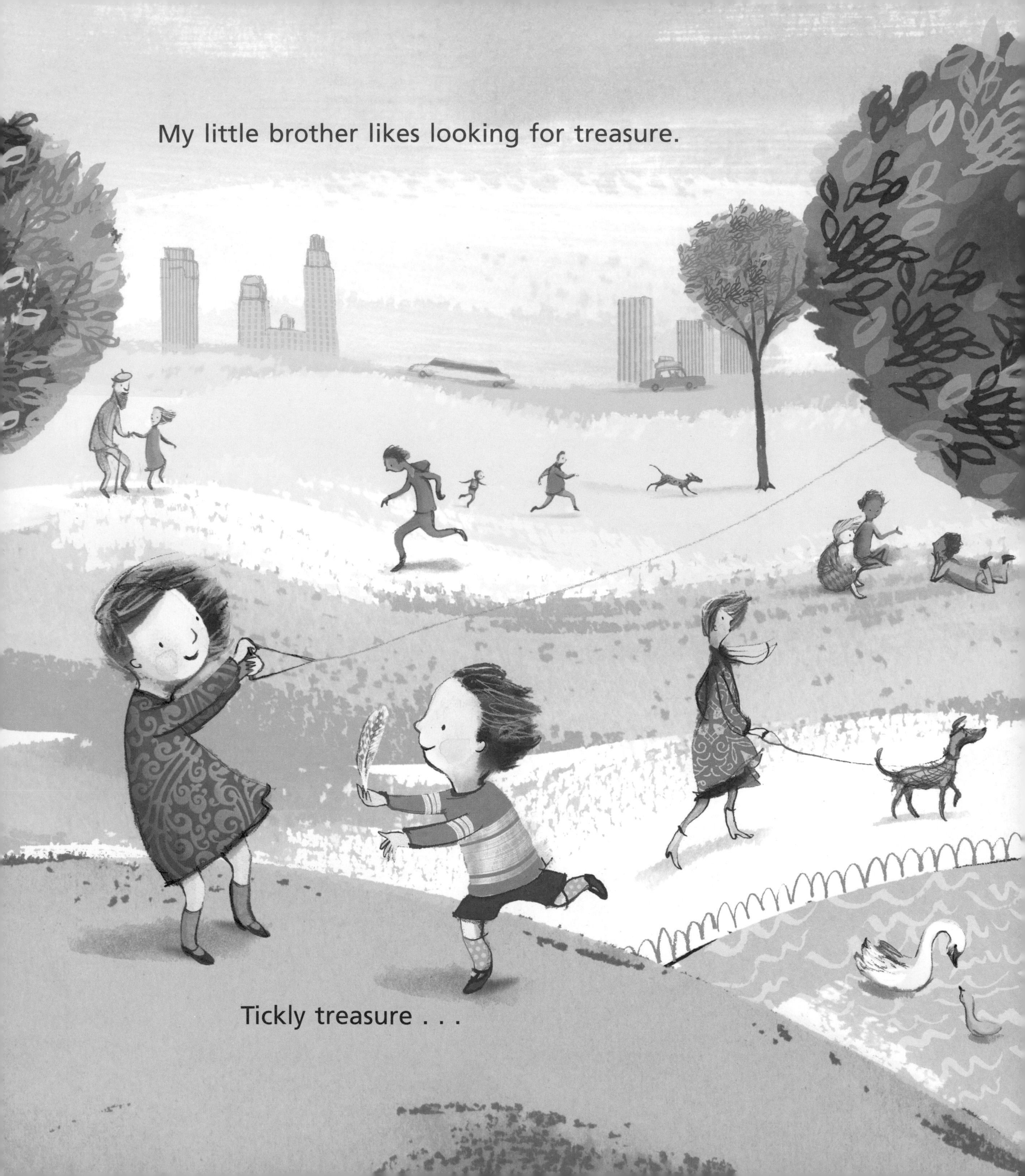

Tickly treasure . . .

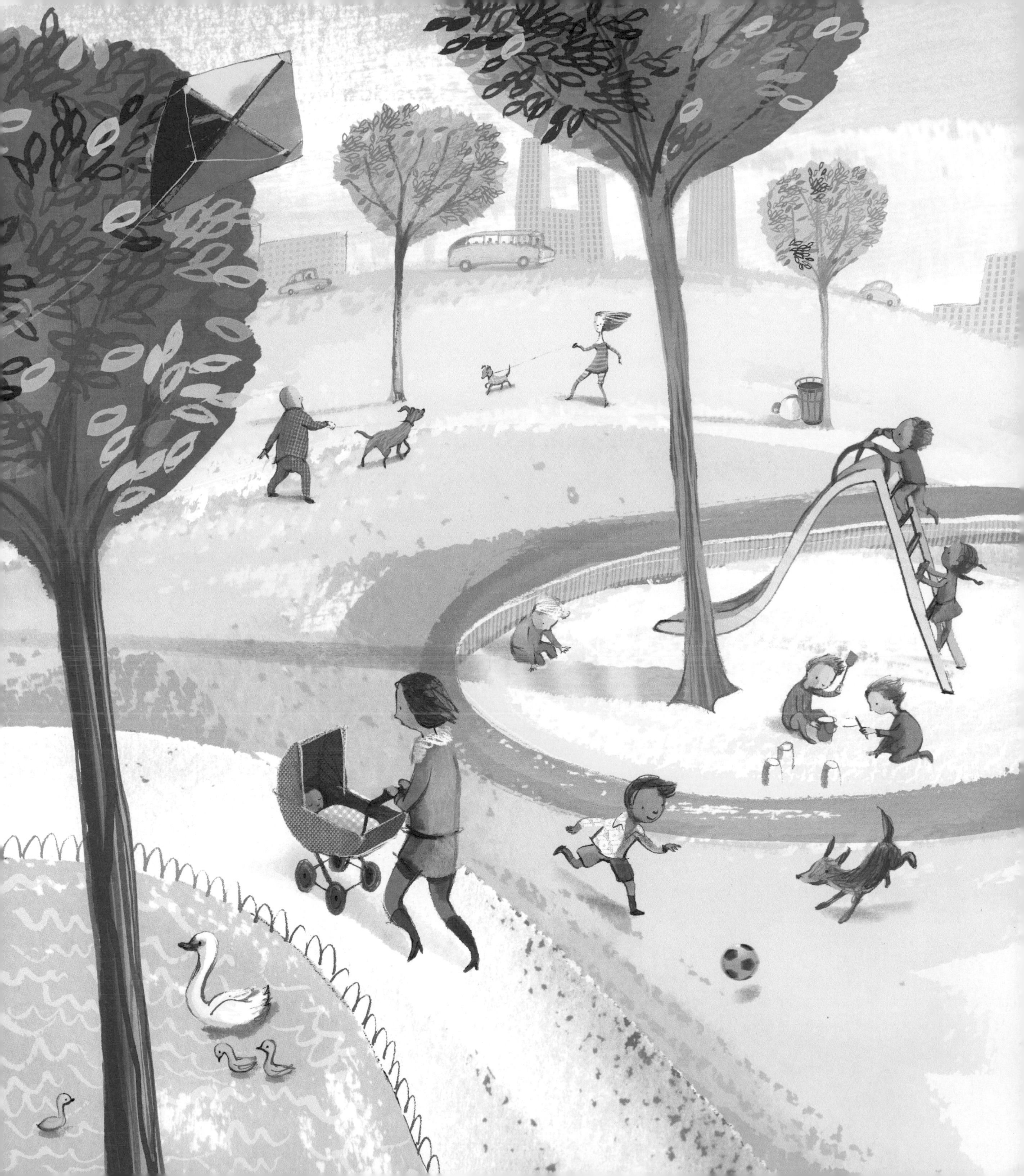

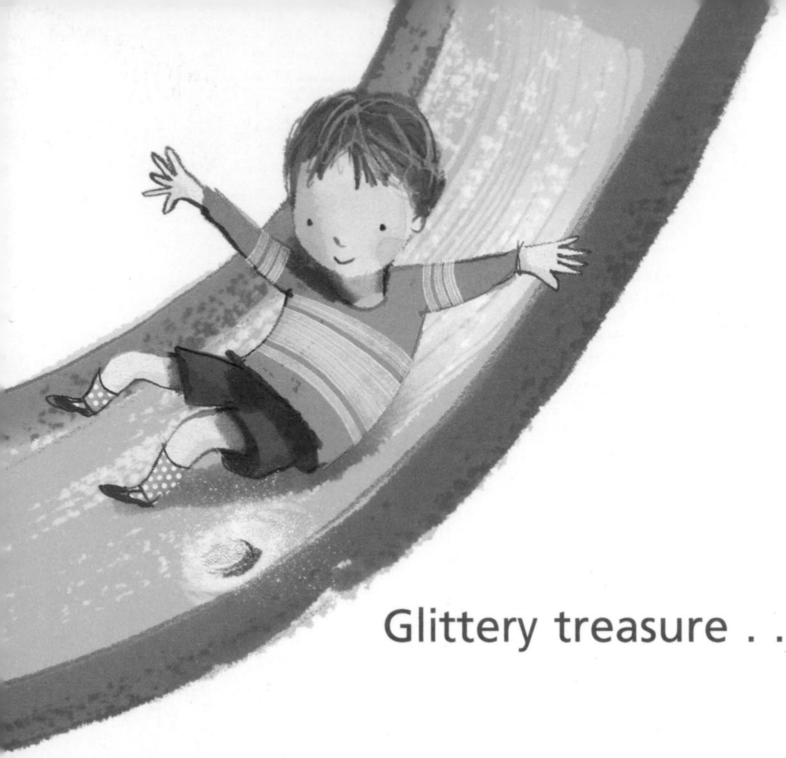

Glittery treasure . . .

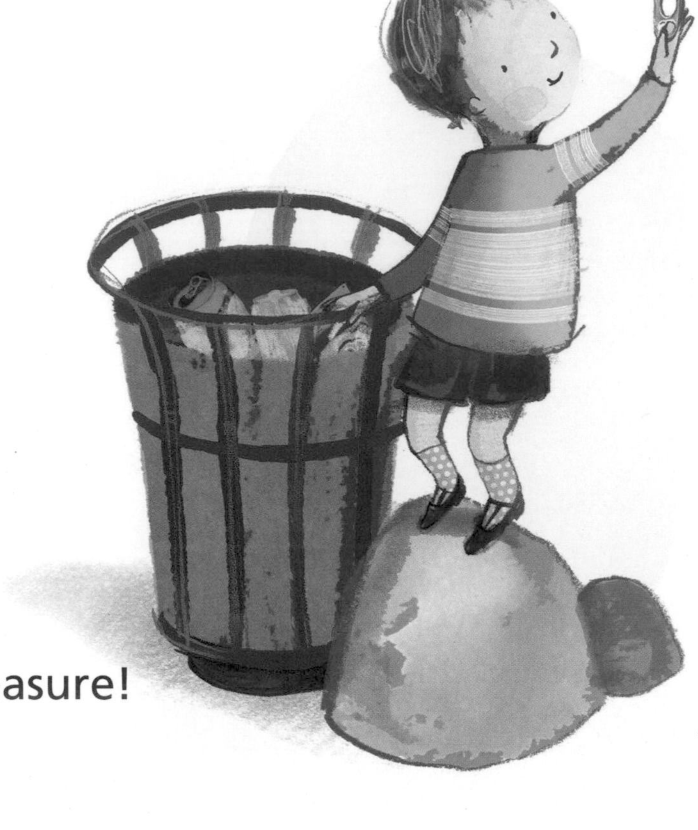

even litter-bin treasure!

But one day he found
something extra special.

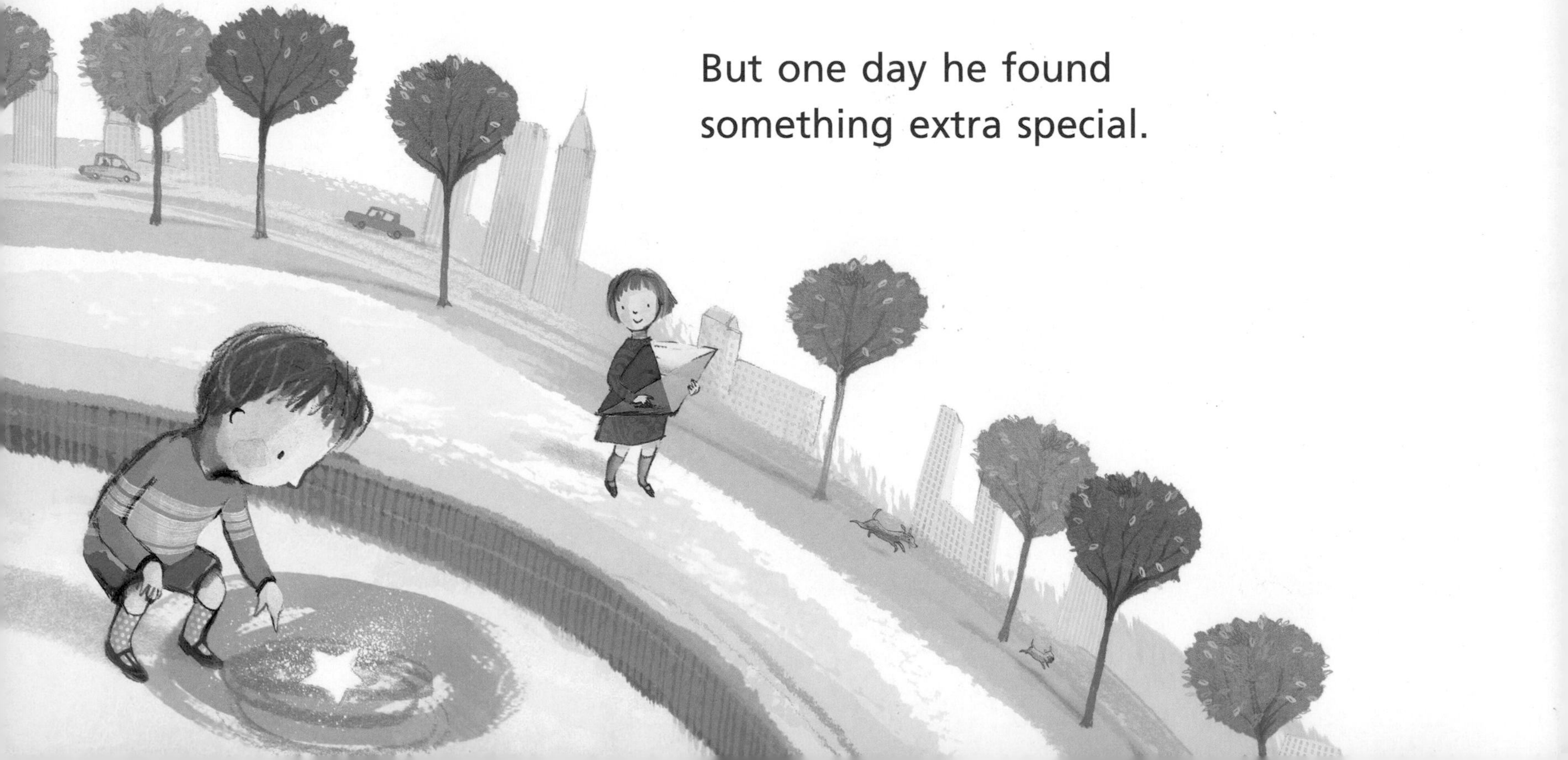

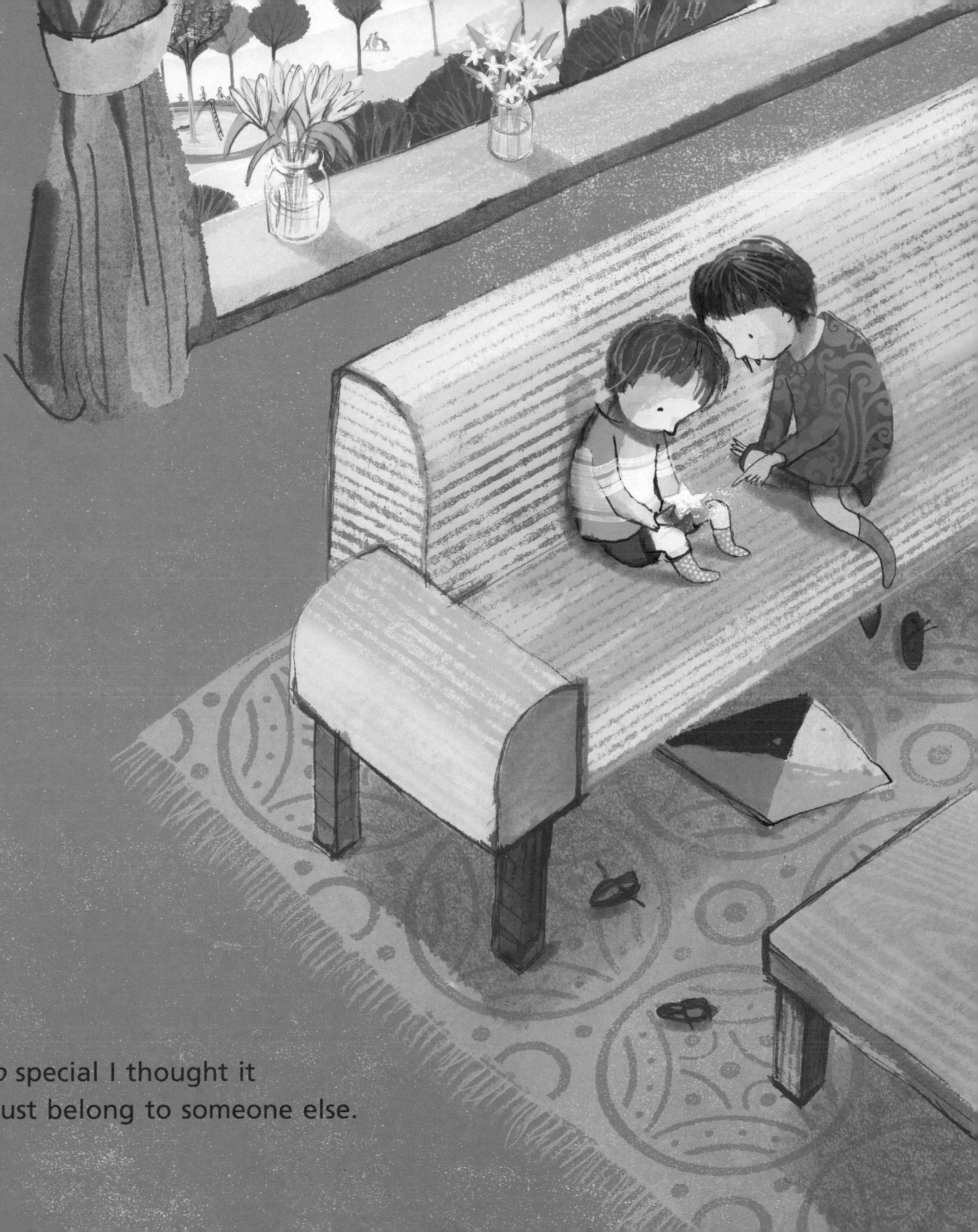

*So* special I thought it
must belong to someone else.

We asked the helpful girl from school.
But she said it wasn't hers.

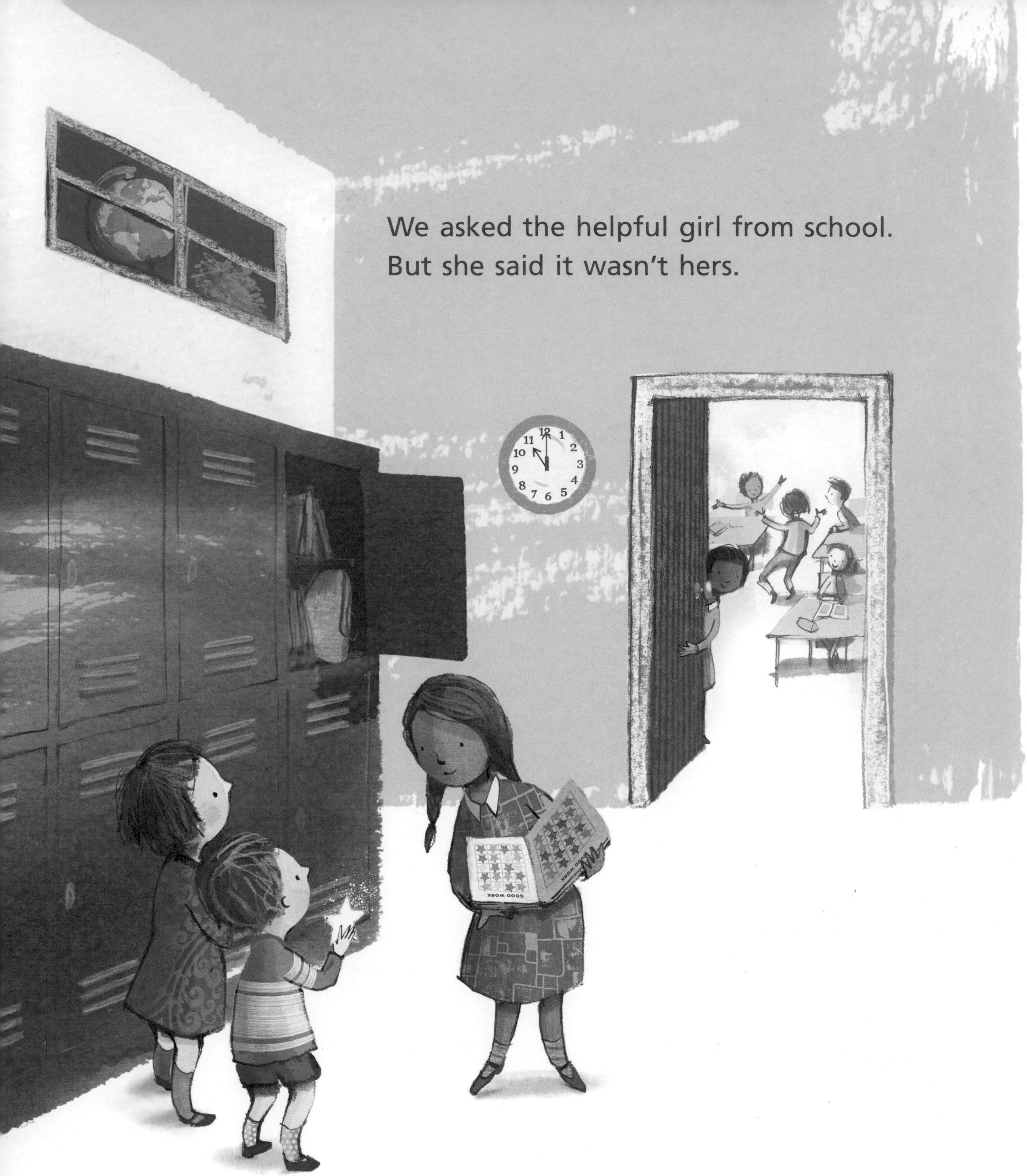
GOOD WORK

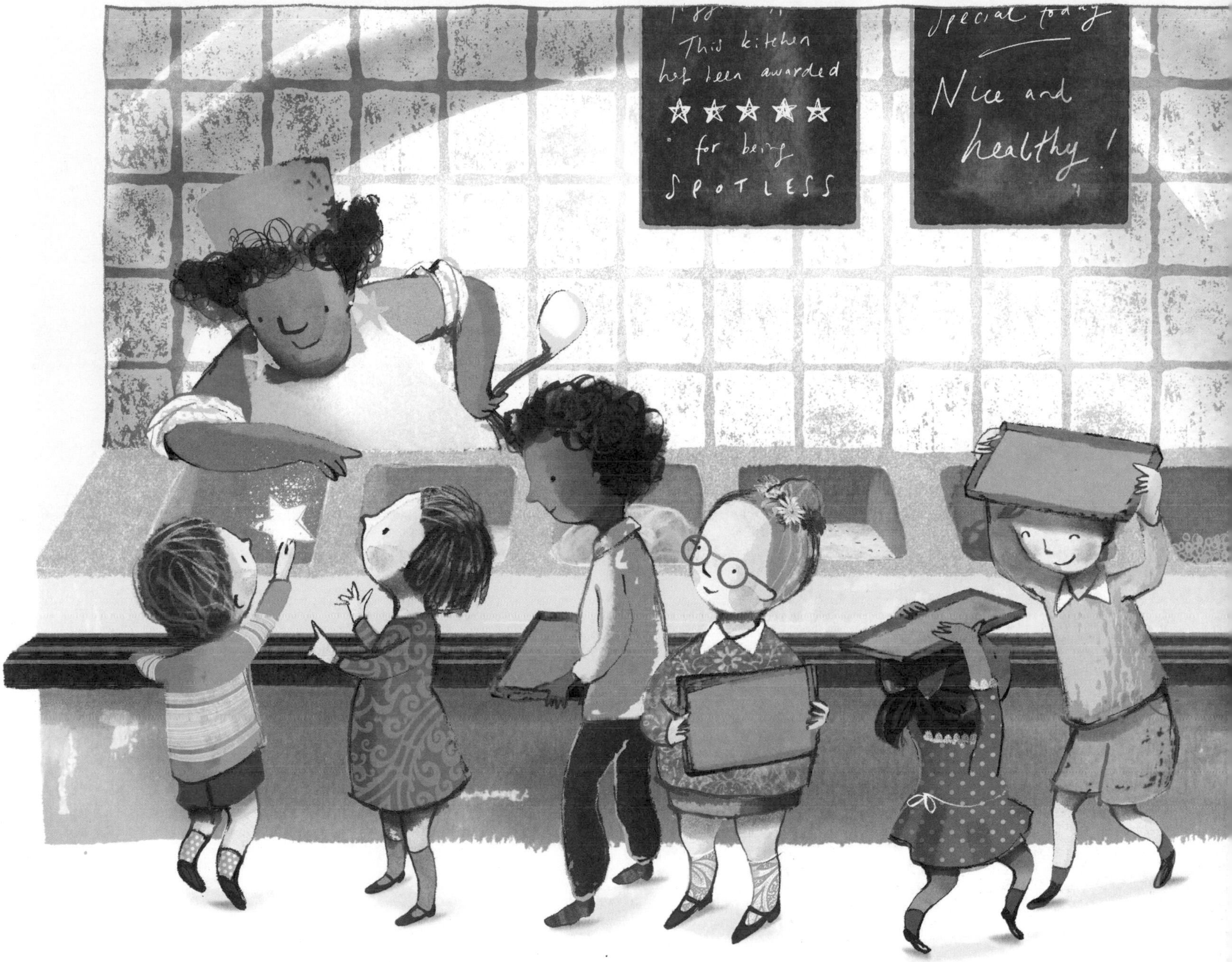
This kitchen
has been awarded
★★★★★
for being
SPOTLESS
Special today
Nice and
healthy!

We showed it to the dinner lady.
But it wasn't hers, either.

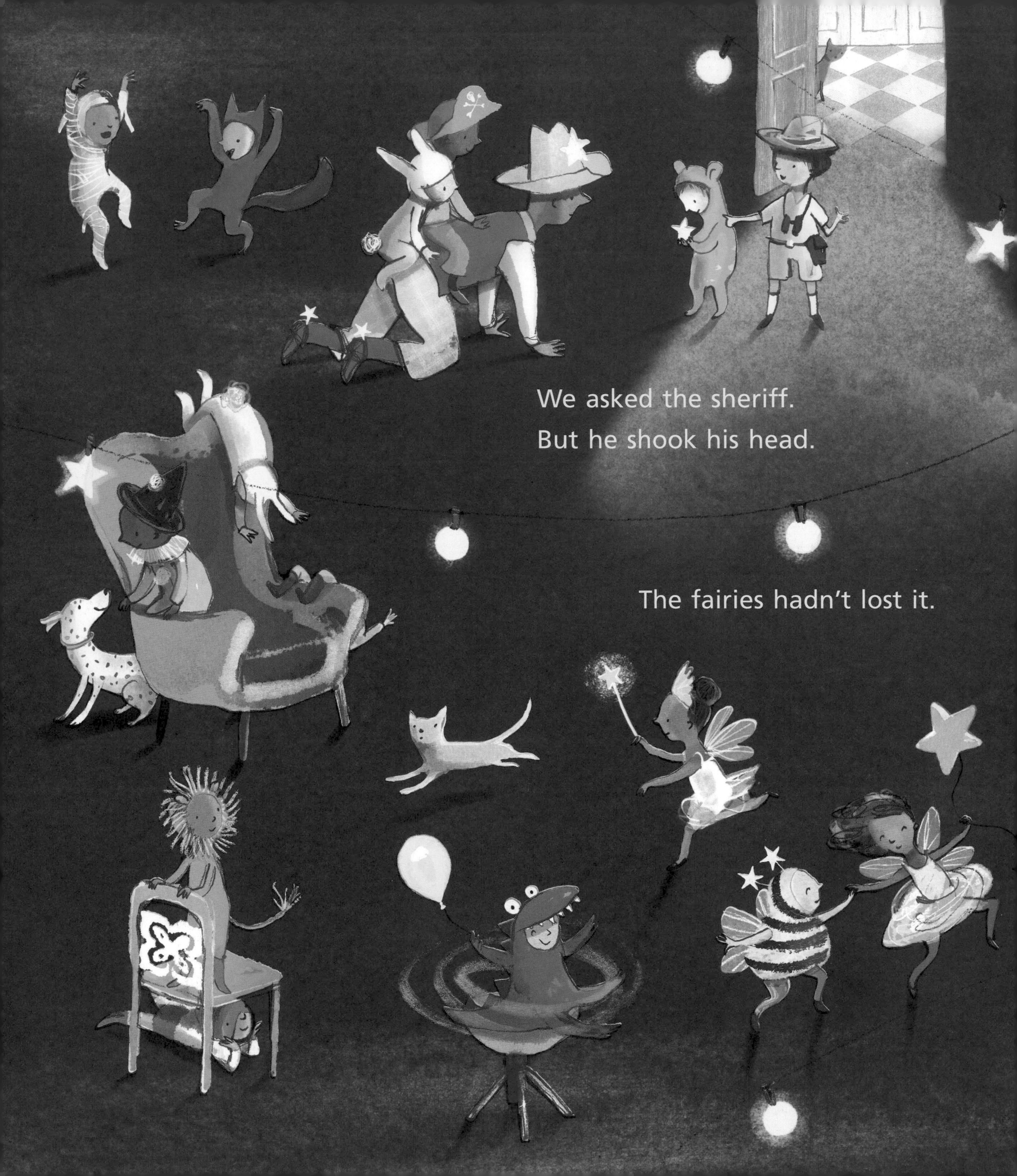

We asked the sheriff.
But he shook his head.

The fairies hadn't lost it.

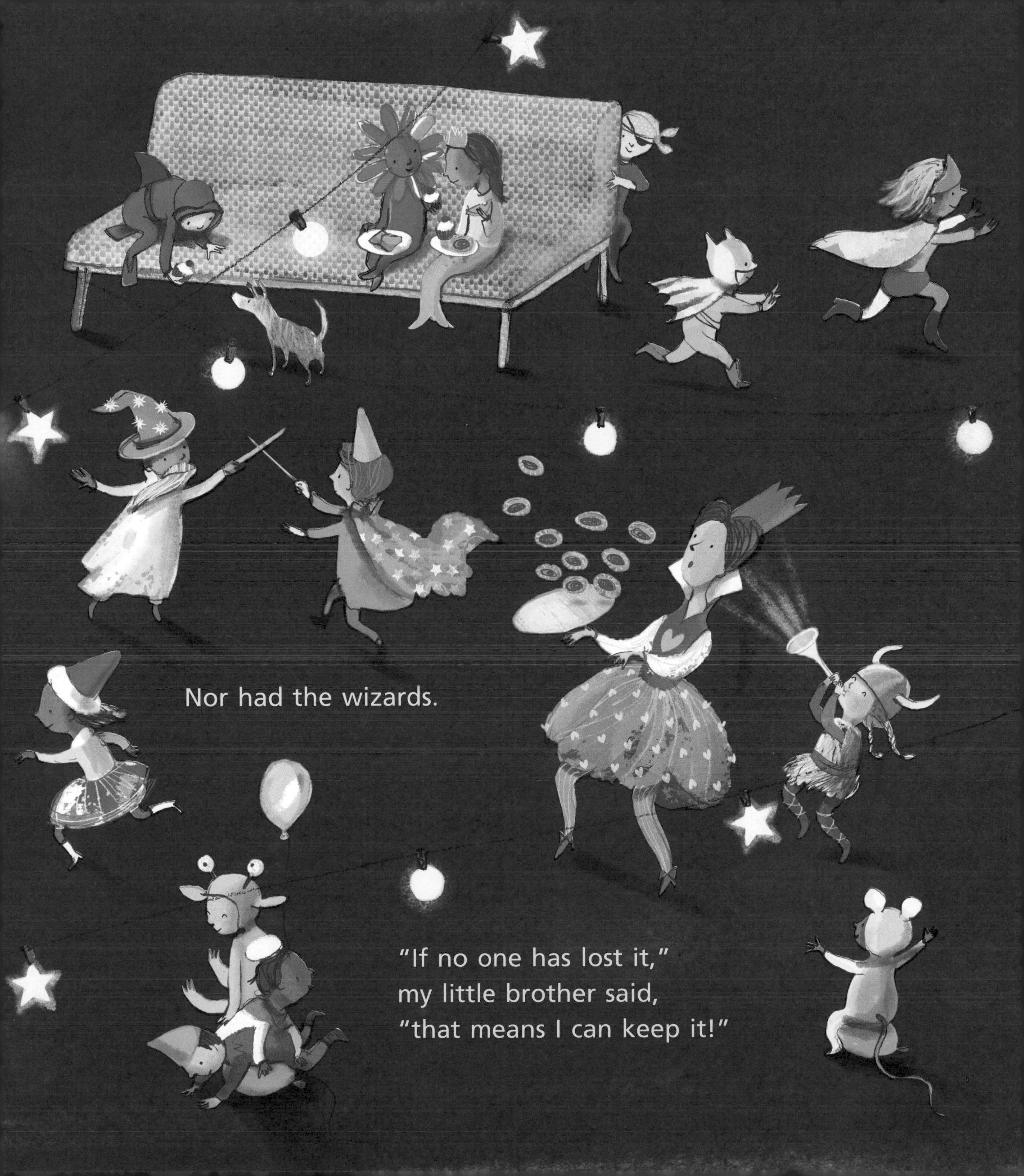

Nor had the wizards.

"If no one has lost it,"
my little brother said,
"that means I can keep it!"

My little brother
loved his new treasure.

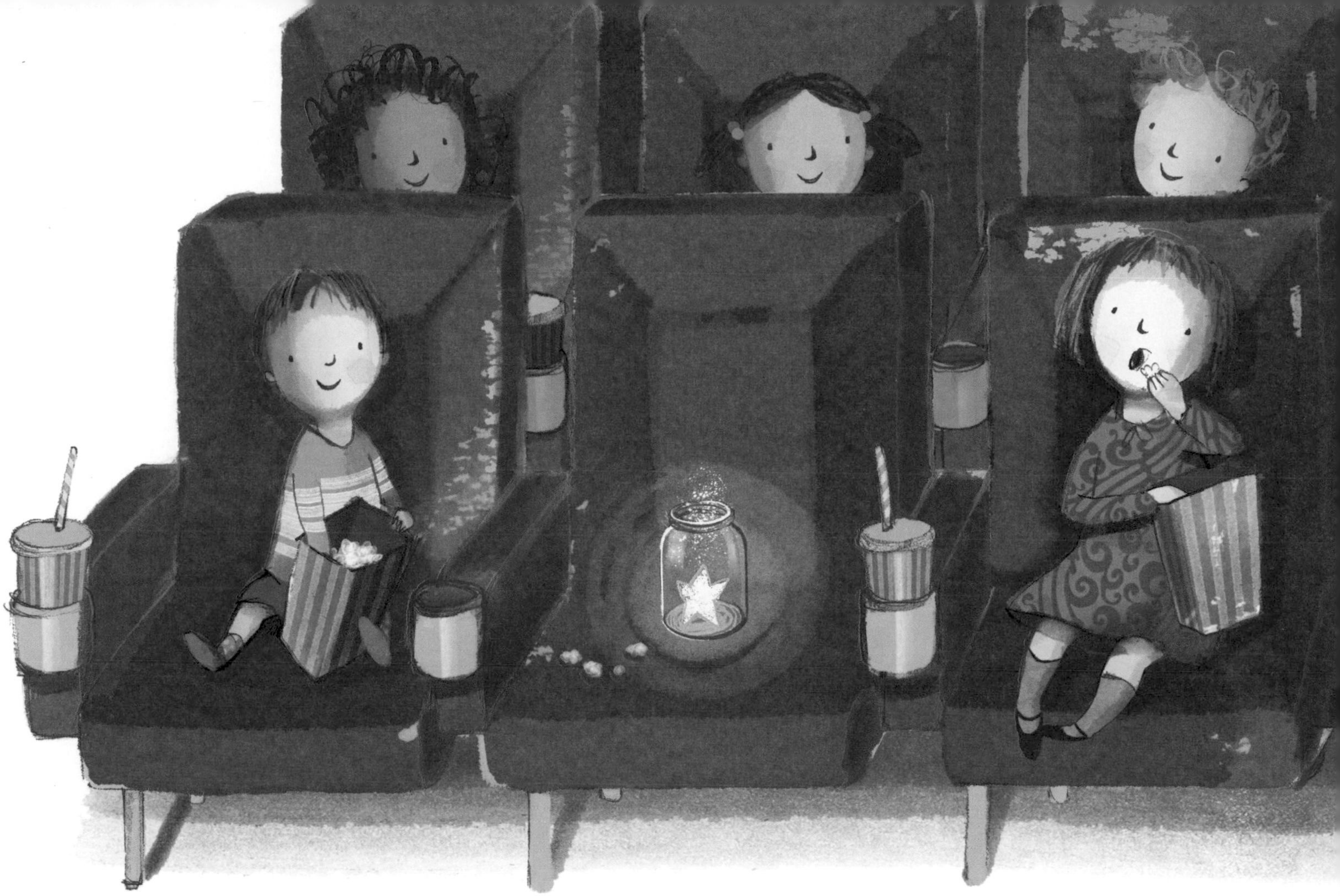

He put it in a jar and
carried it everywhere.

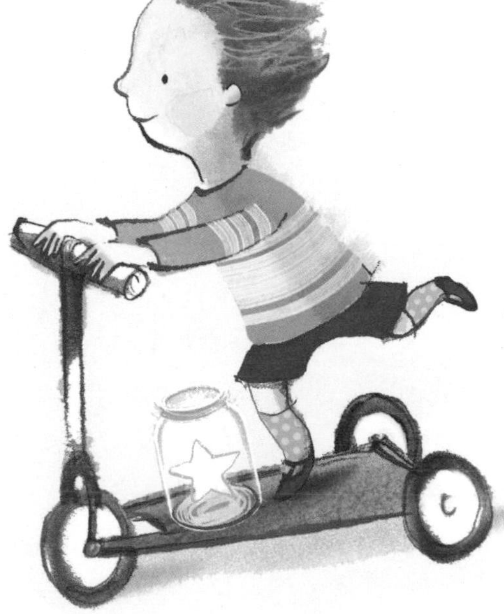

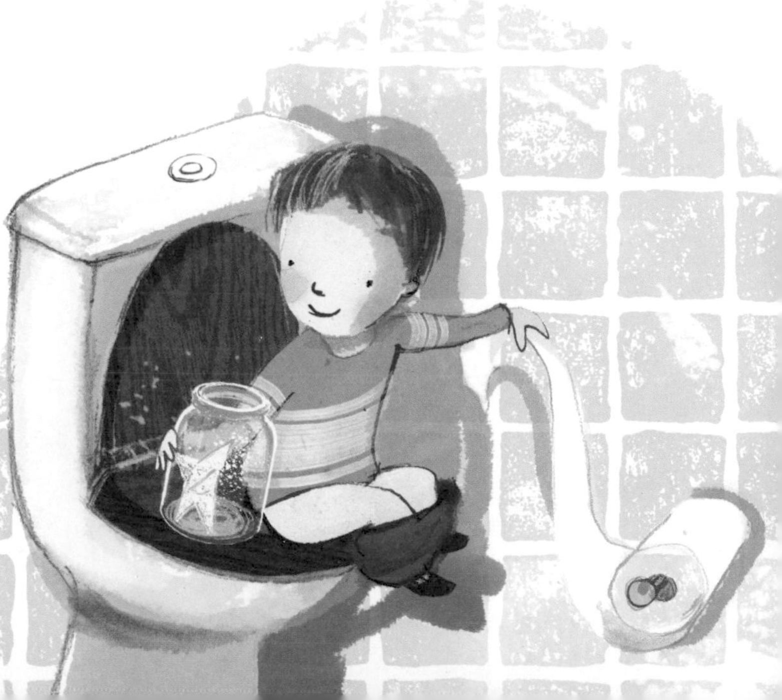

As the day turned into night, the little treasure got shinier.
But it didn't look happy.

Then my little brother spotted something.
Up high, in the dark, dark sky, there was a message!

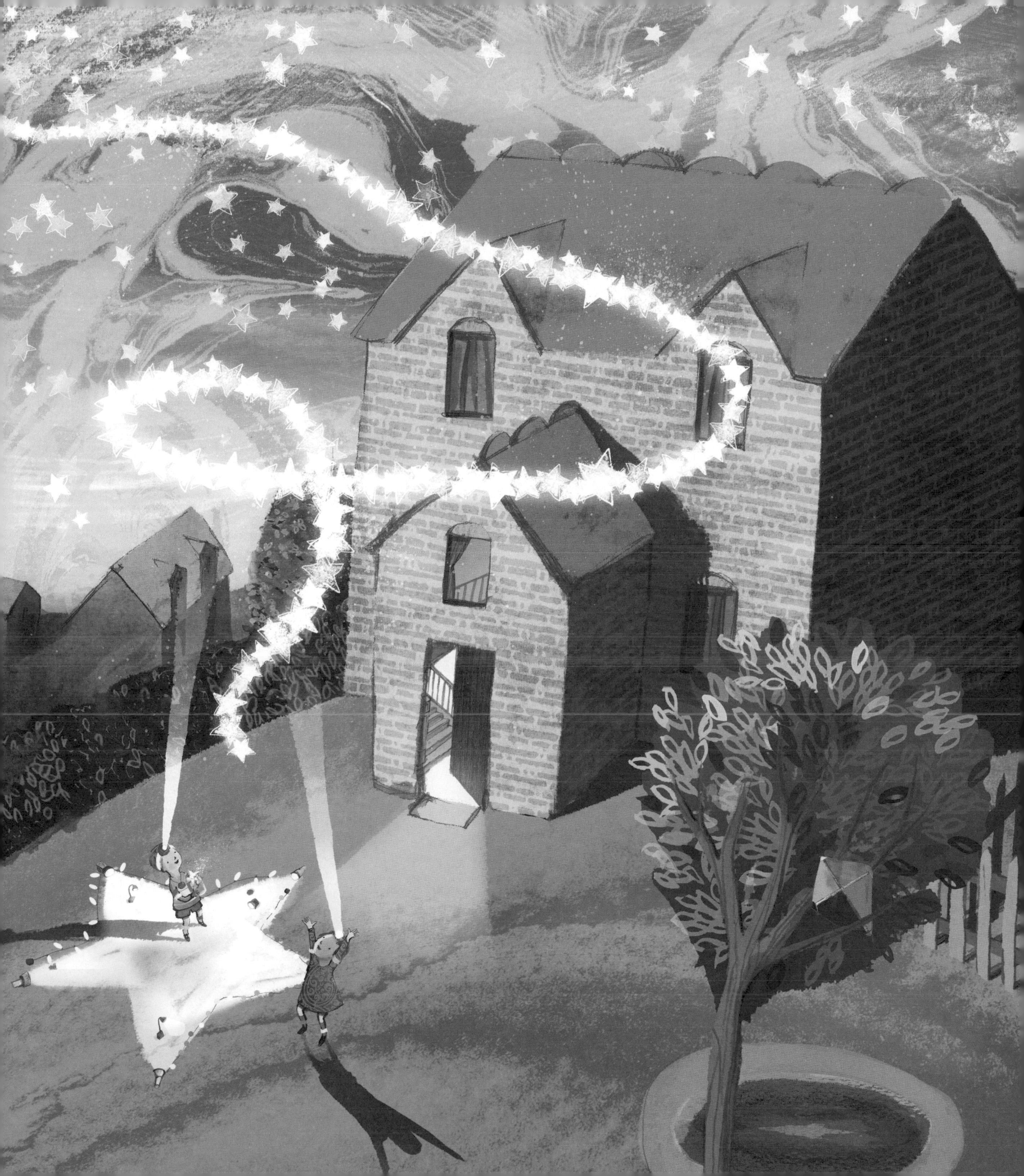

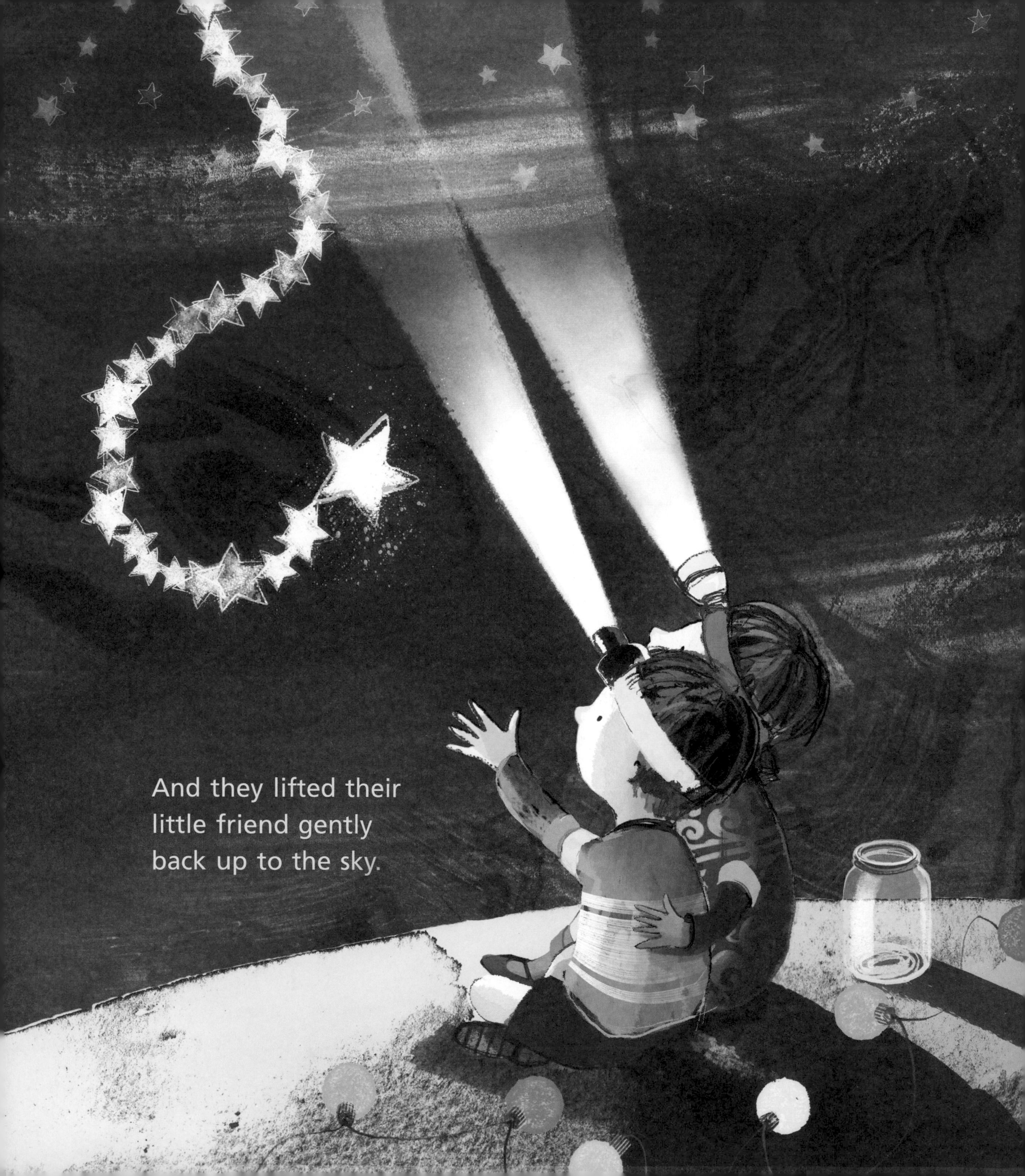

And they lifted their
little friend gently
back up to the sky.

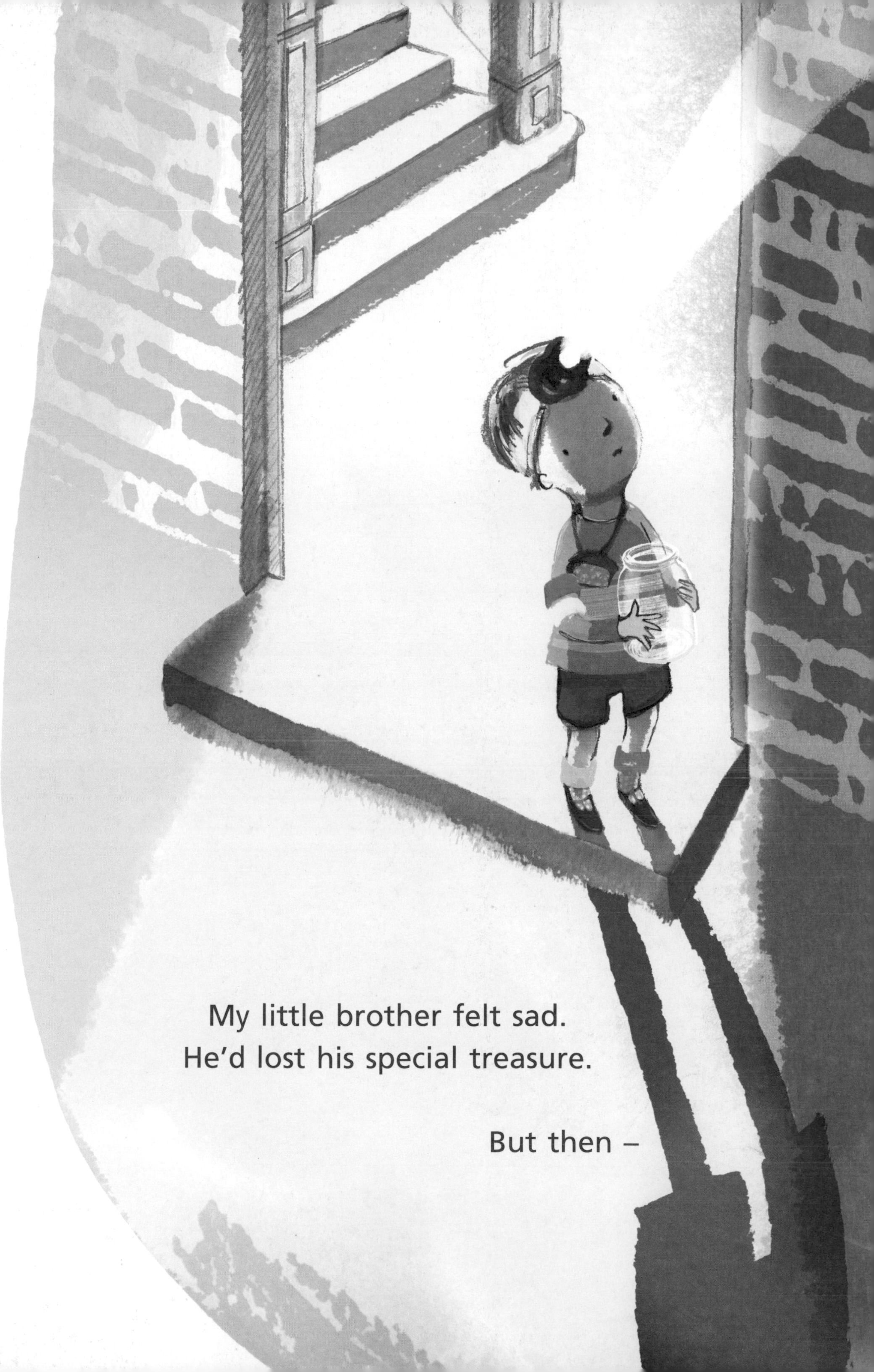

My little brother felt sad.
He'd lost his special treasure.

But then –

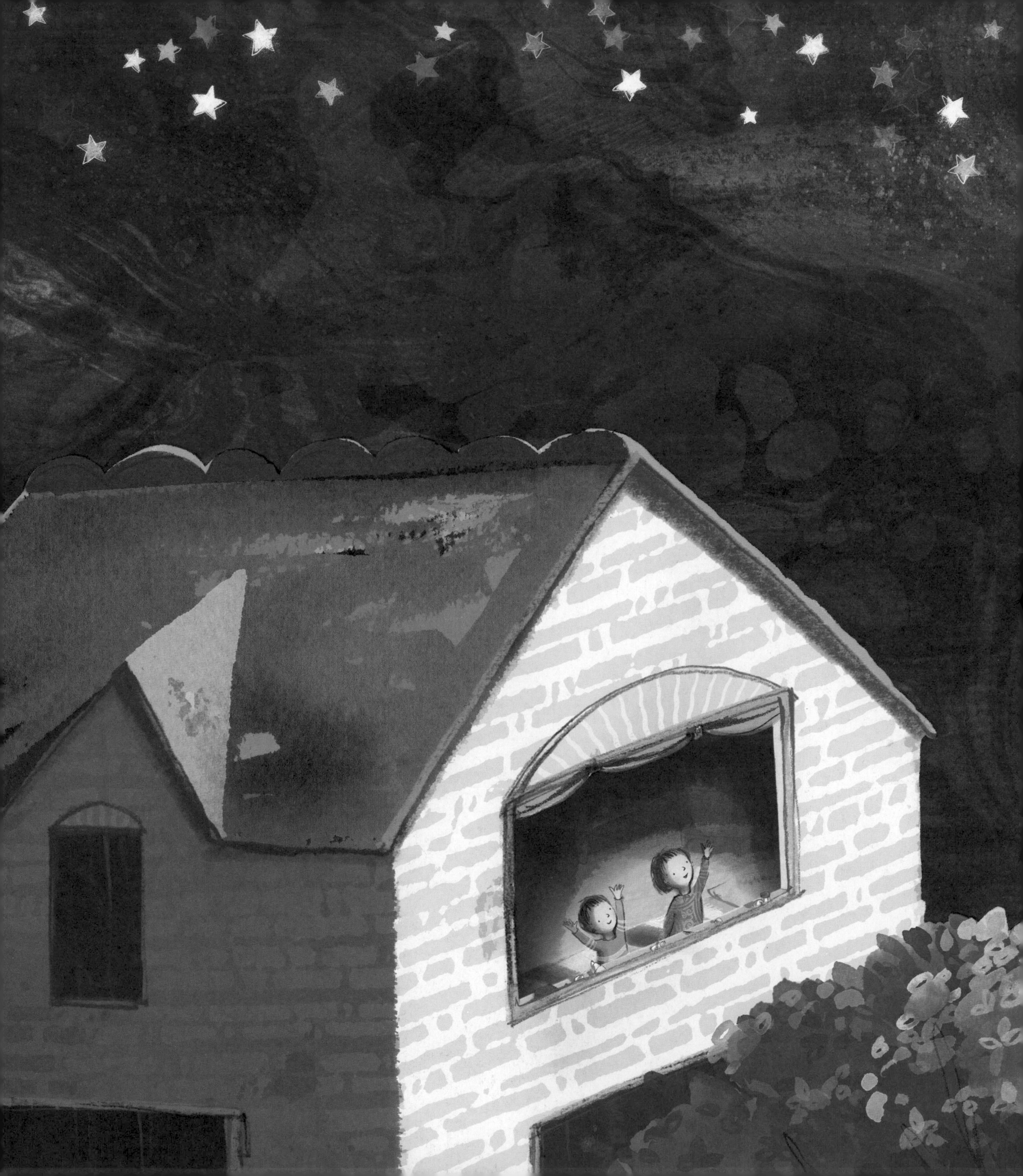

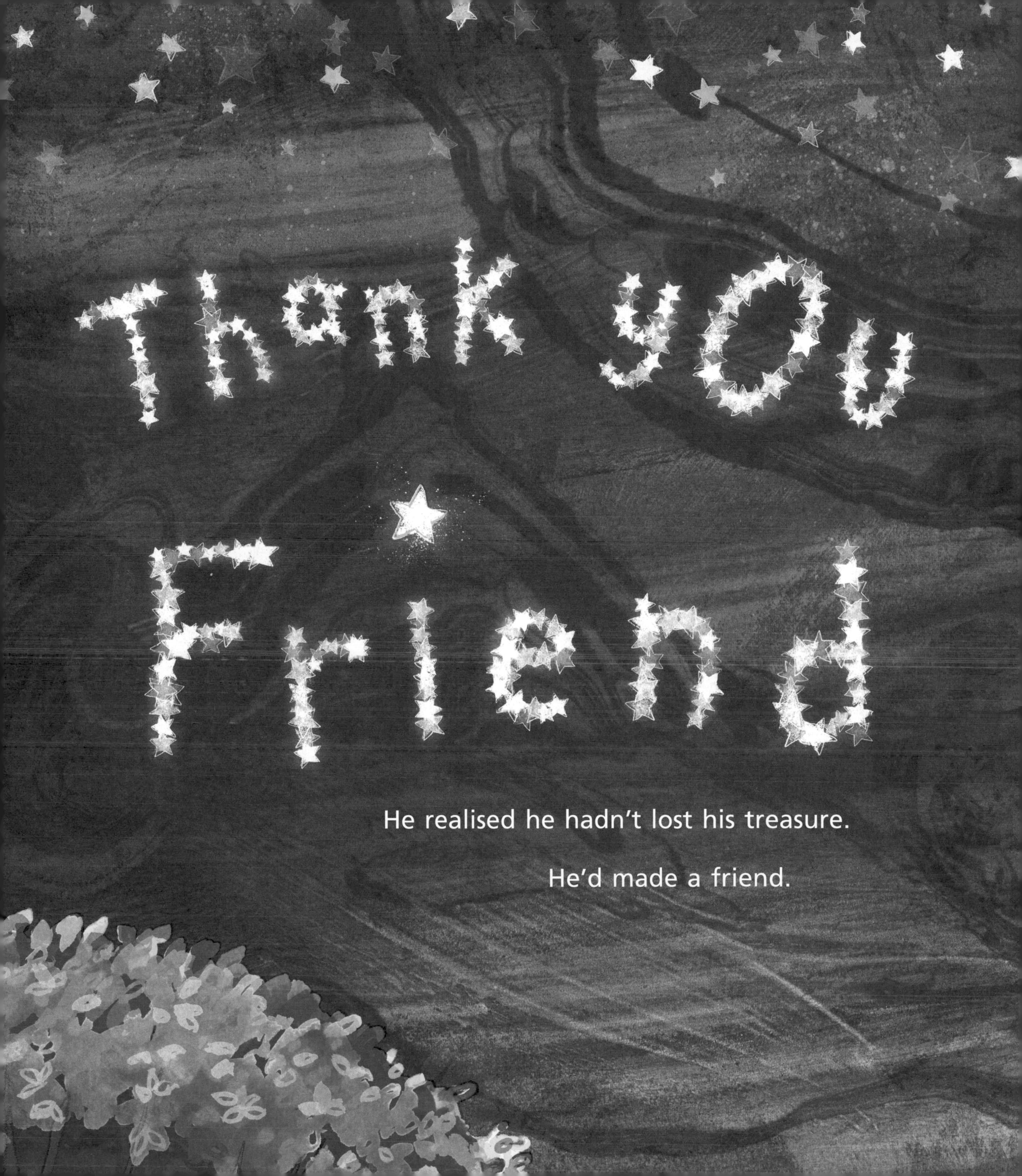
Thank you
Friend

He realised he hadn't lost his treasure.

He'd made a friend.

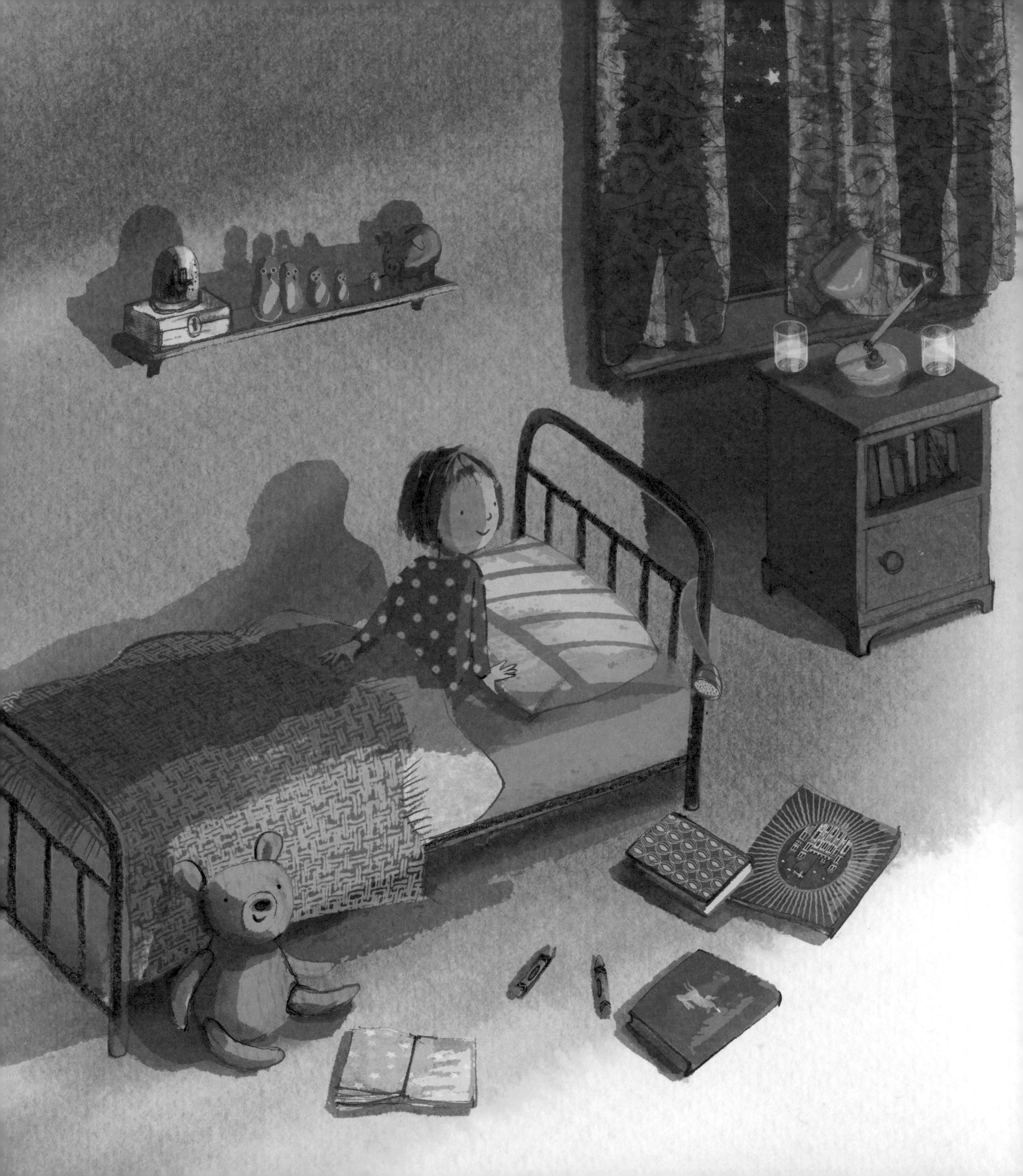

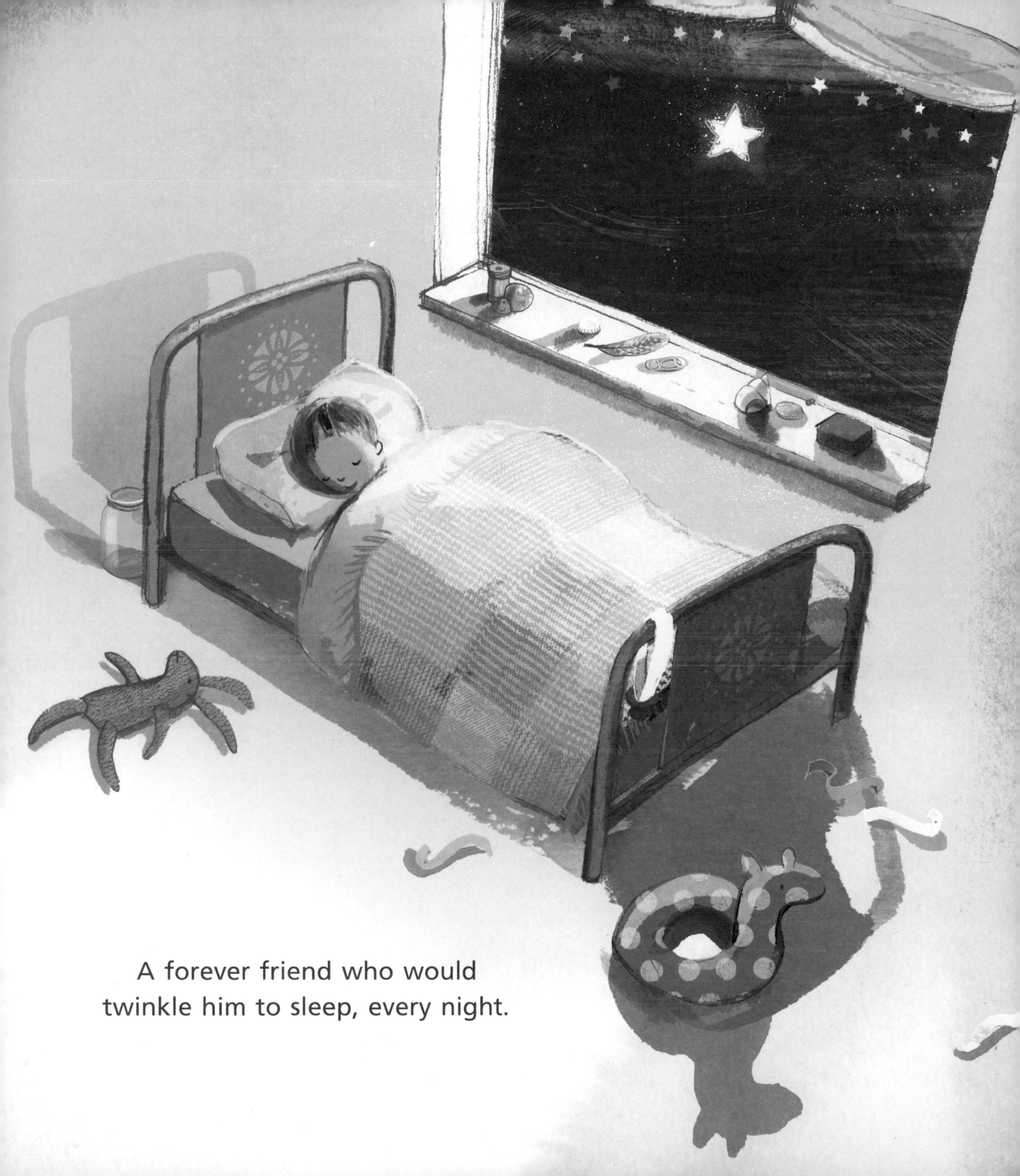

A forever friend who would
twinkle him to sleep, every night.

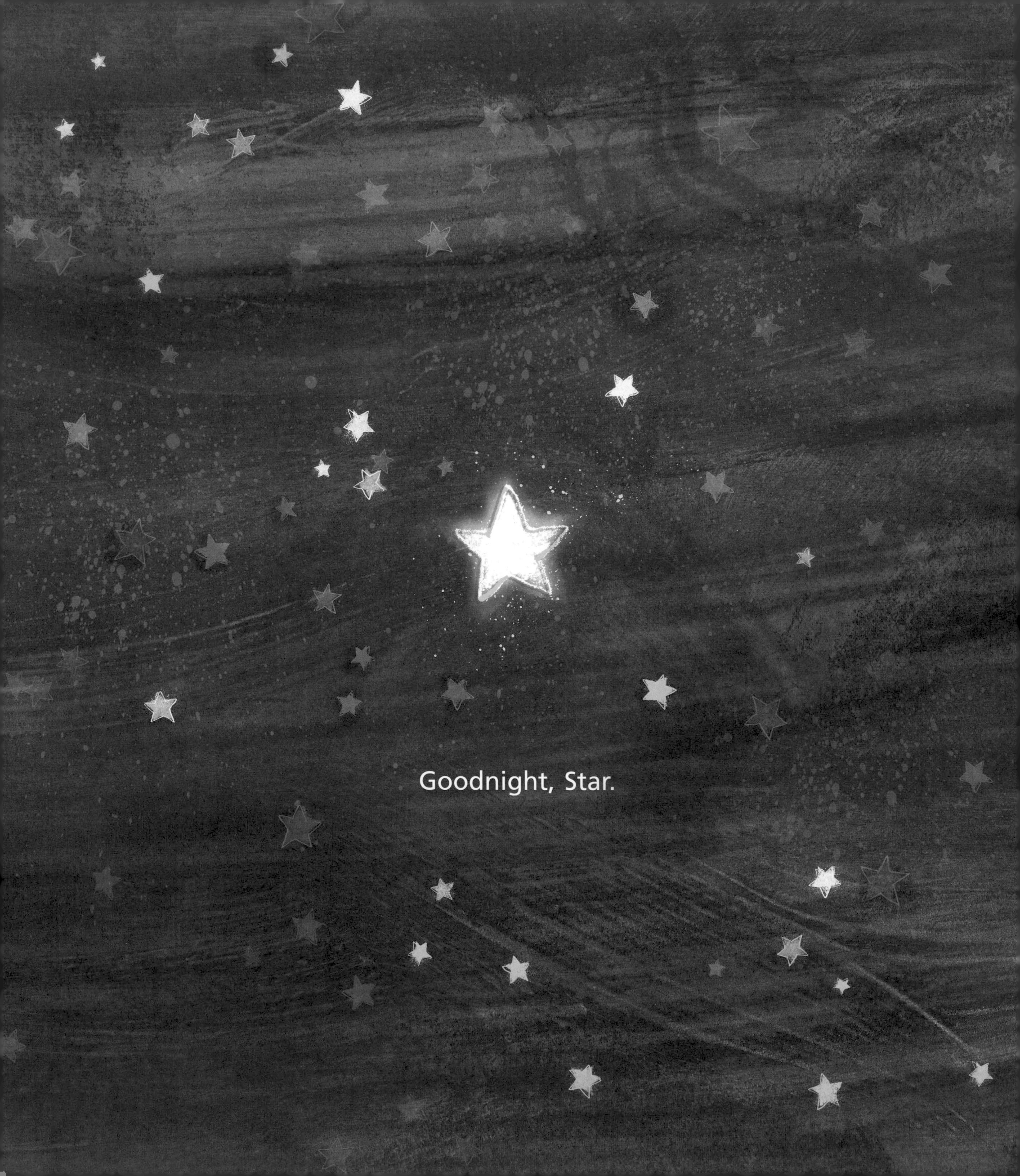

Goodnight, Star.

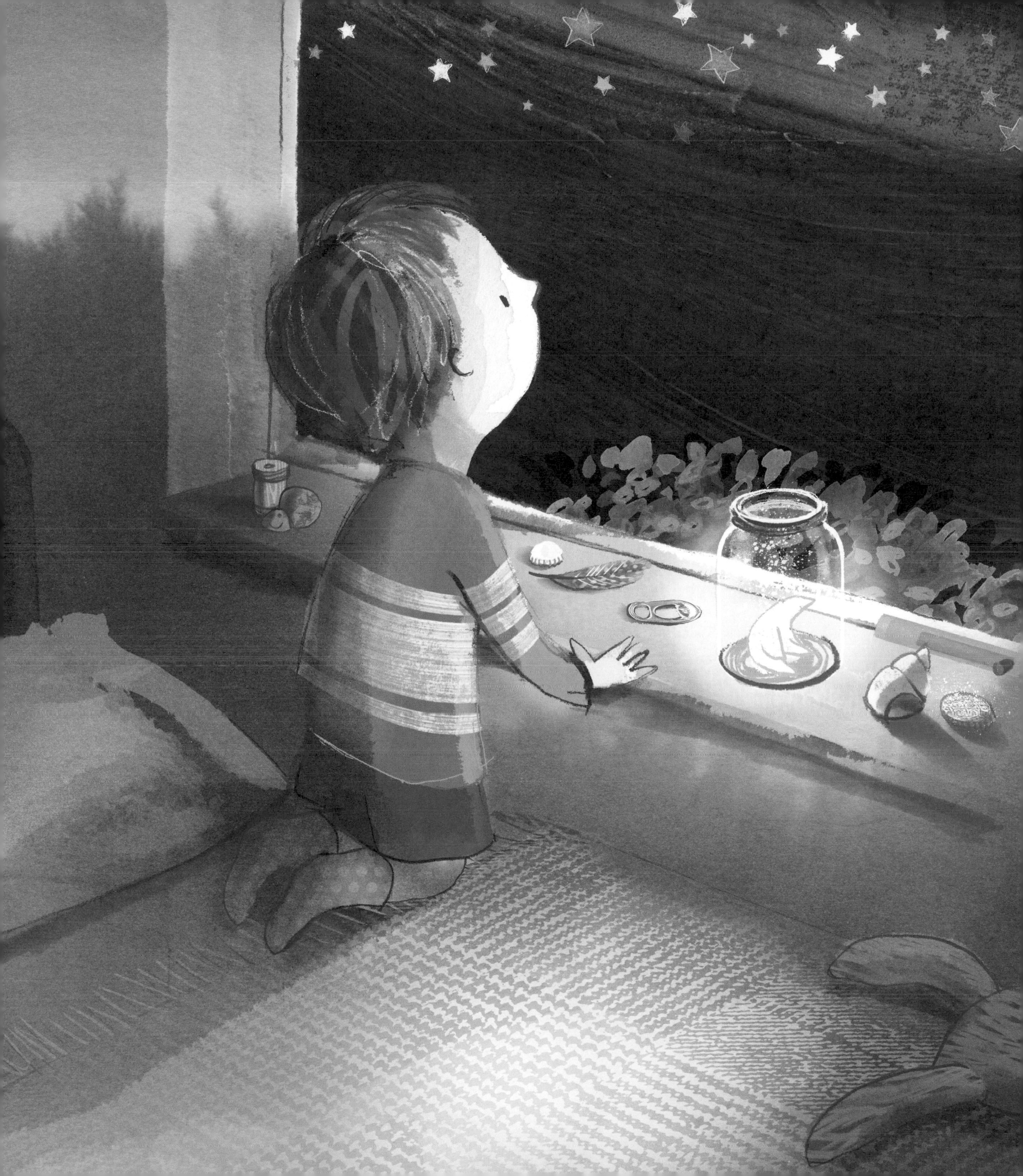

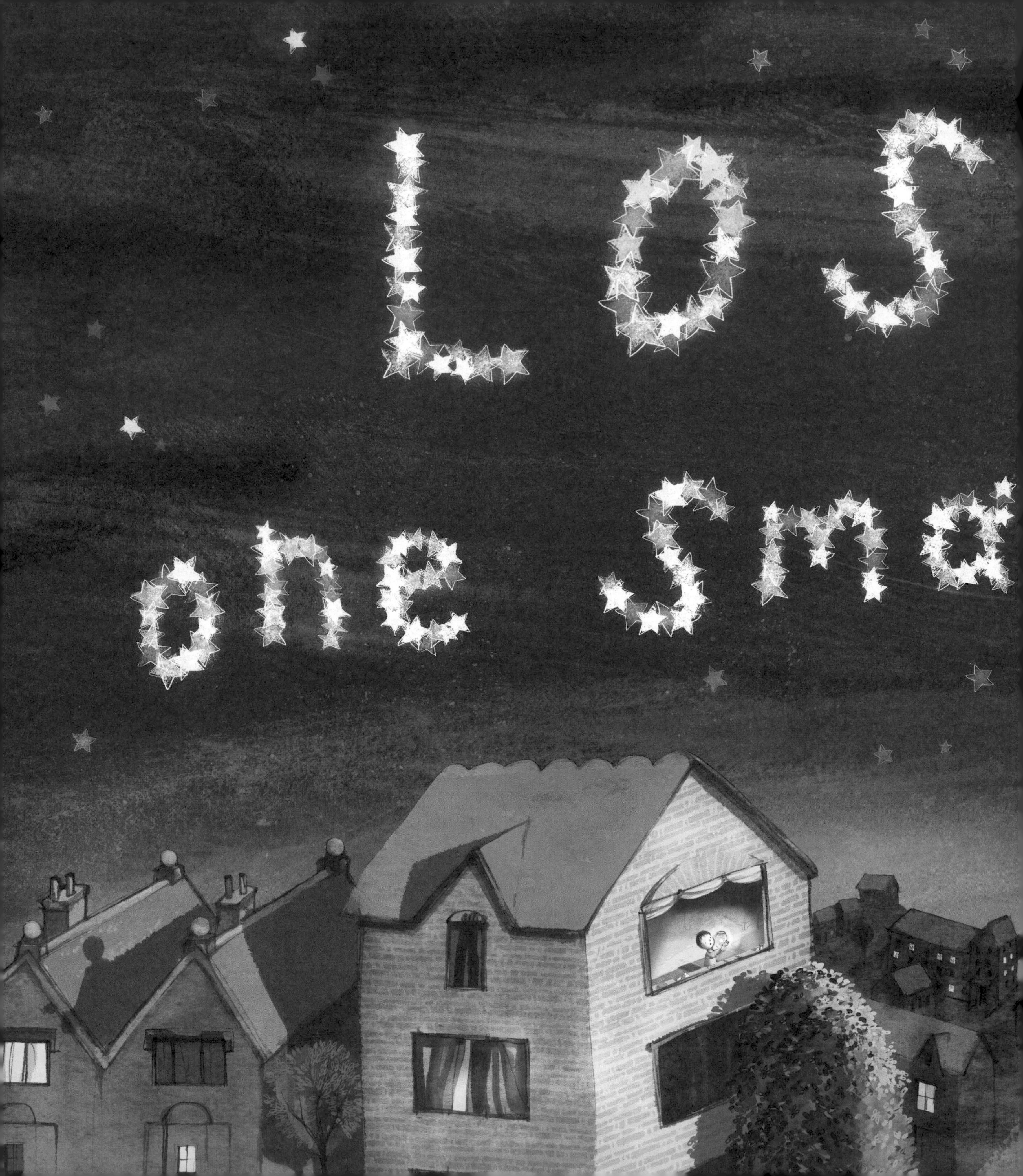
LO
one sma

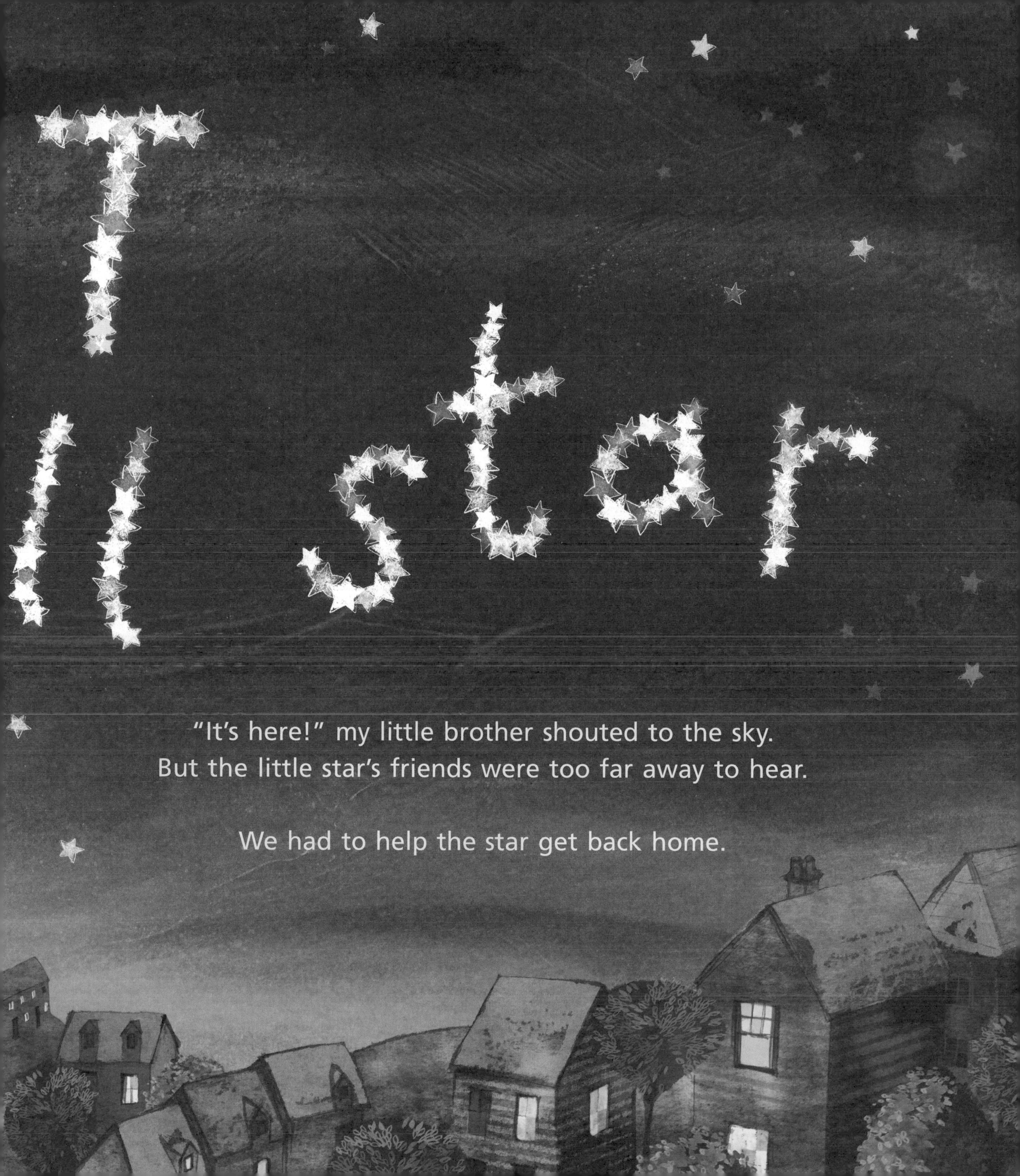
T
ll star

"It's here!" my little brother shouted to the sky.
But the little star's friends were too far away to hear.

We had to help the star get back home.

We tried climbing up high,

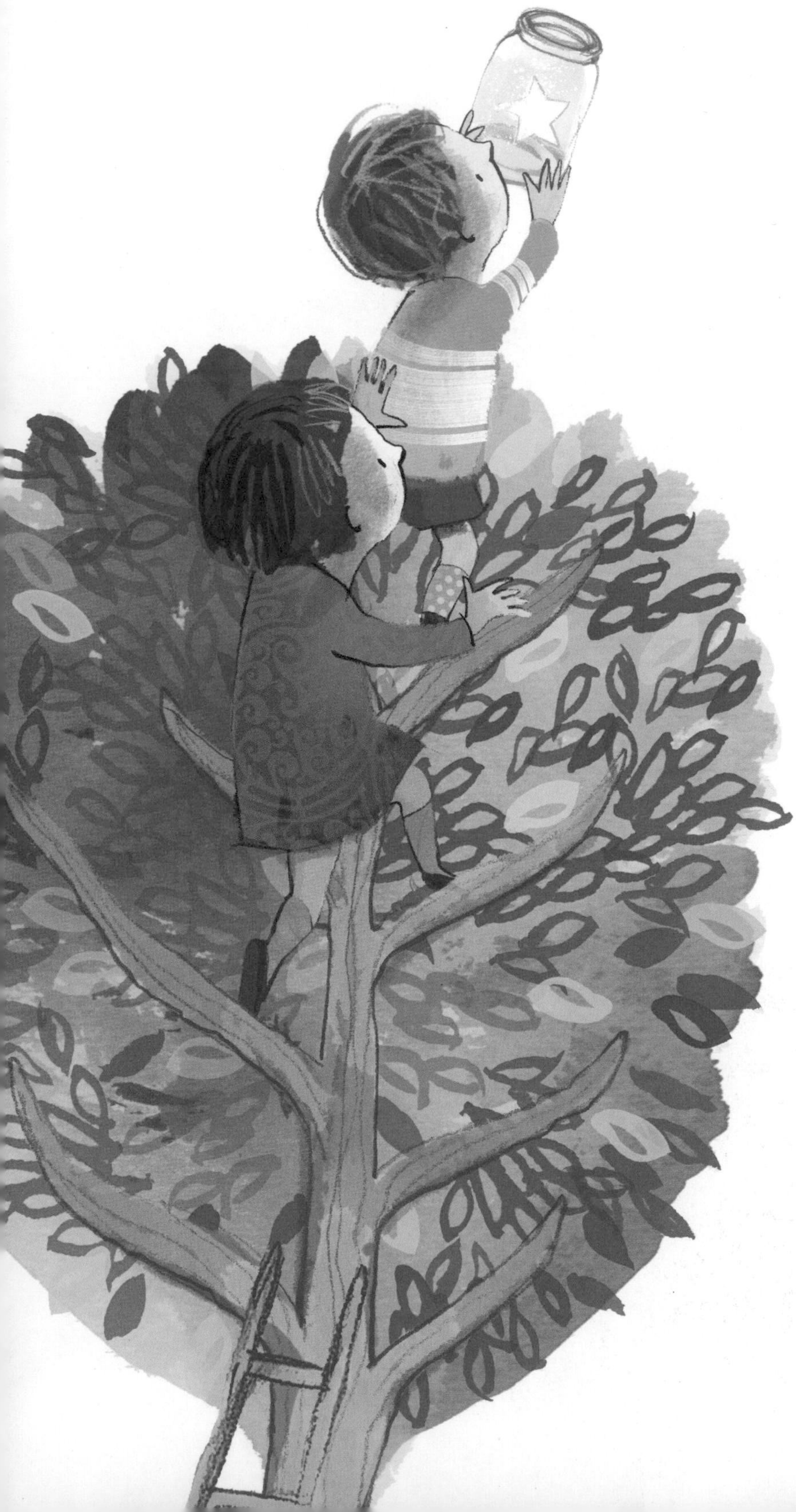

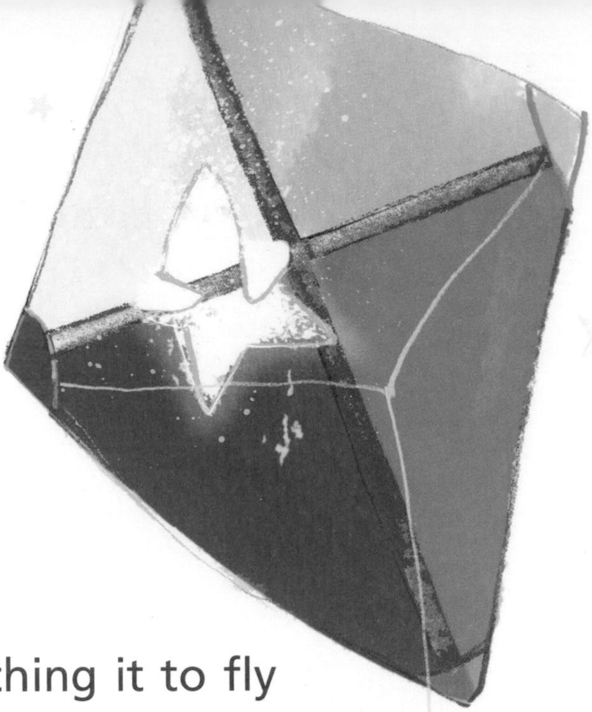

teaching it to fly

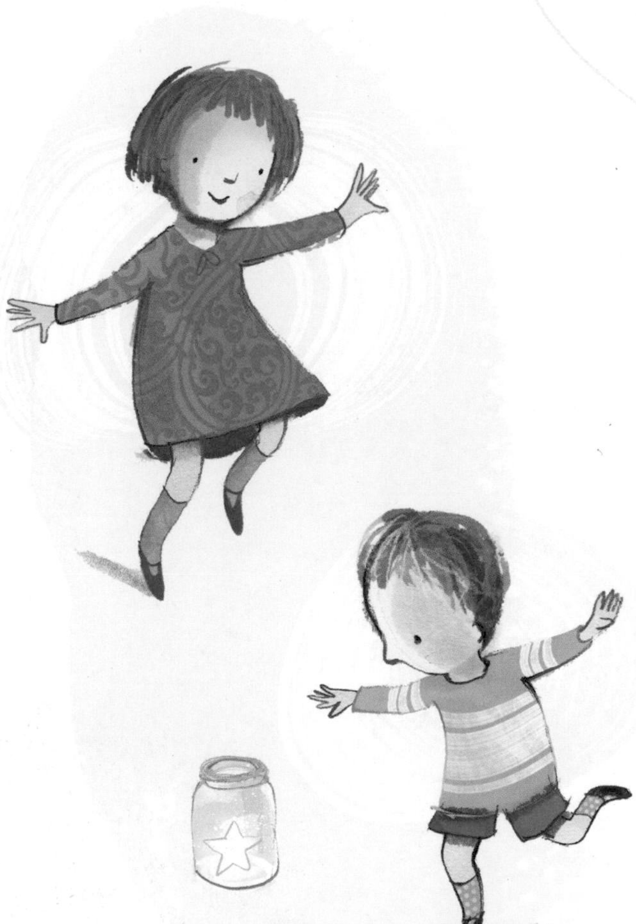

and bouncing the star back up to the sky.

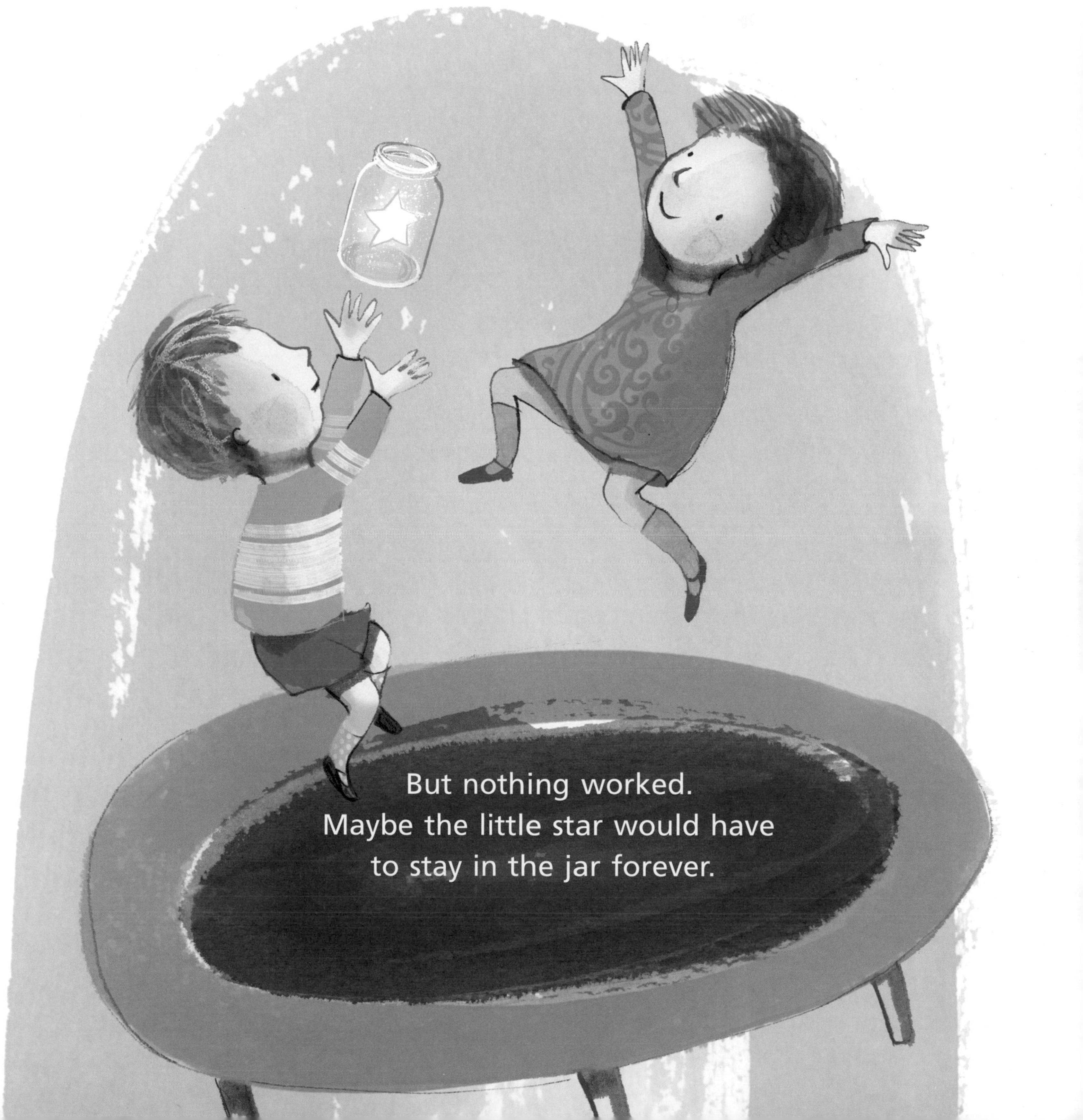

But nothing worked.
Maybe the little star would have
to stay in the jar forever.

Then an idea popped into my head.
I raced indoors and looked in every
cupboard and every drawer.

I found flashlights and fairy lights.

Book lamps and bike lights.

Arm bands and head torches.

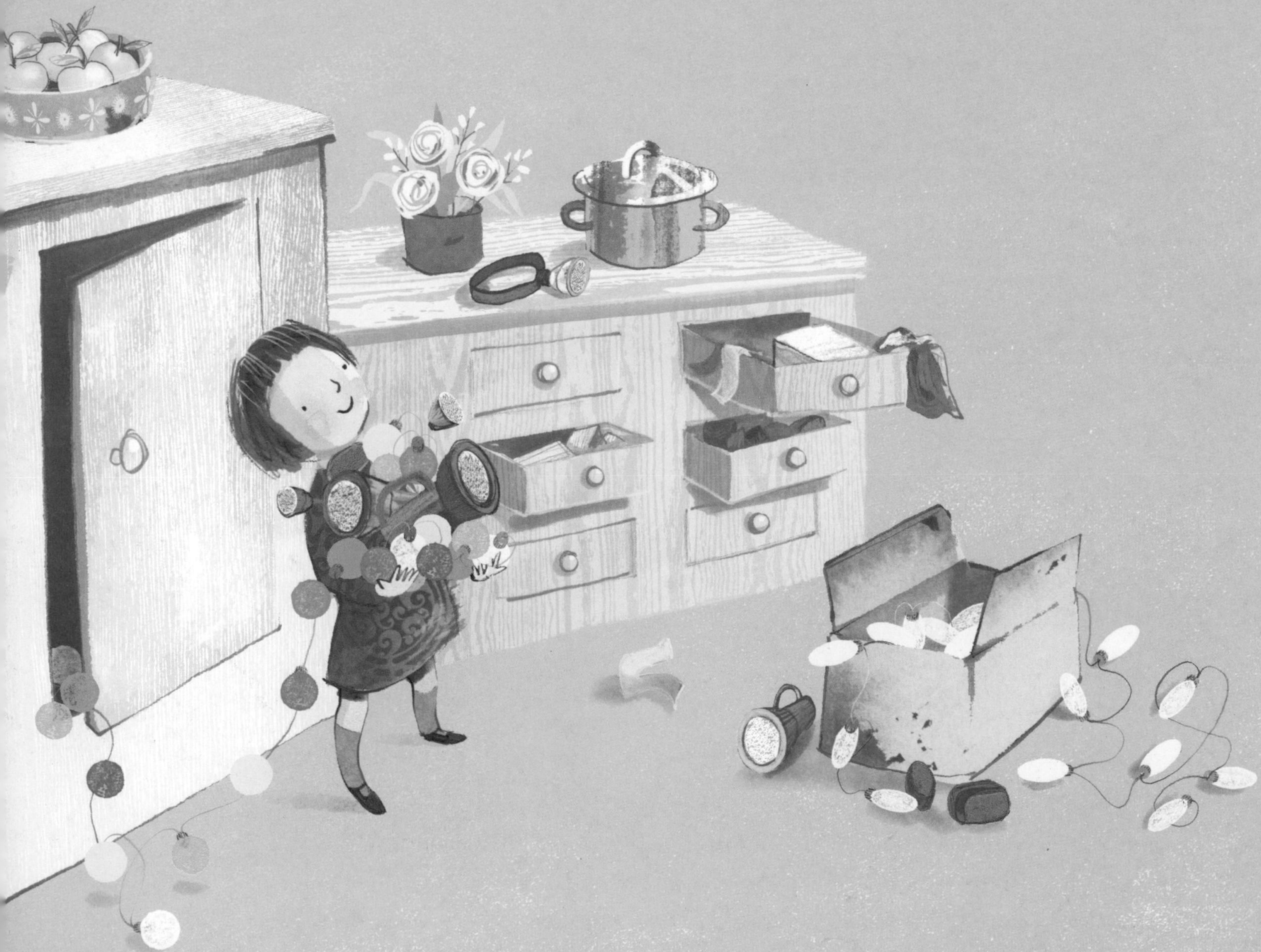

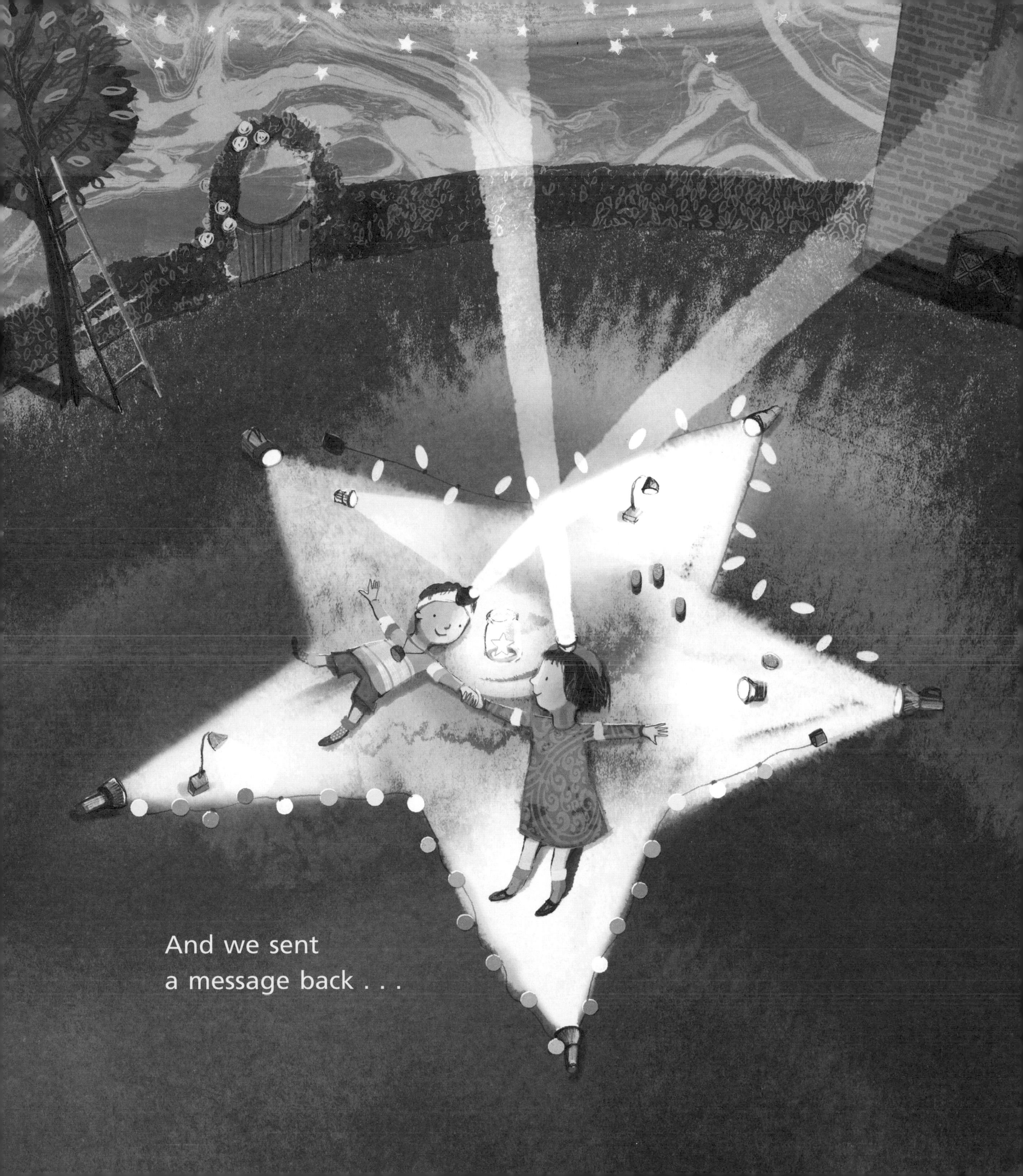

And we sent
a message back . . .

Then the sky began to crackle.

And fizz.

And the stars joined together and made a long swirly, whirly, sparkly silver chain. All the way down to our garden . . .

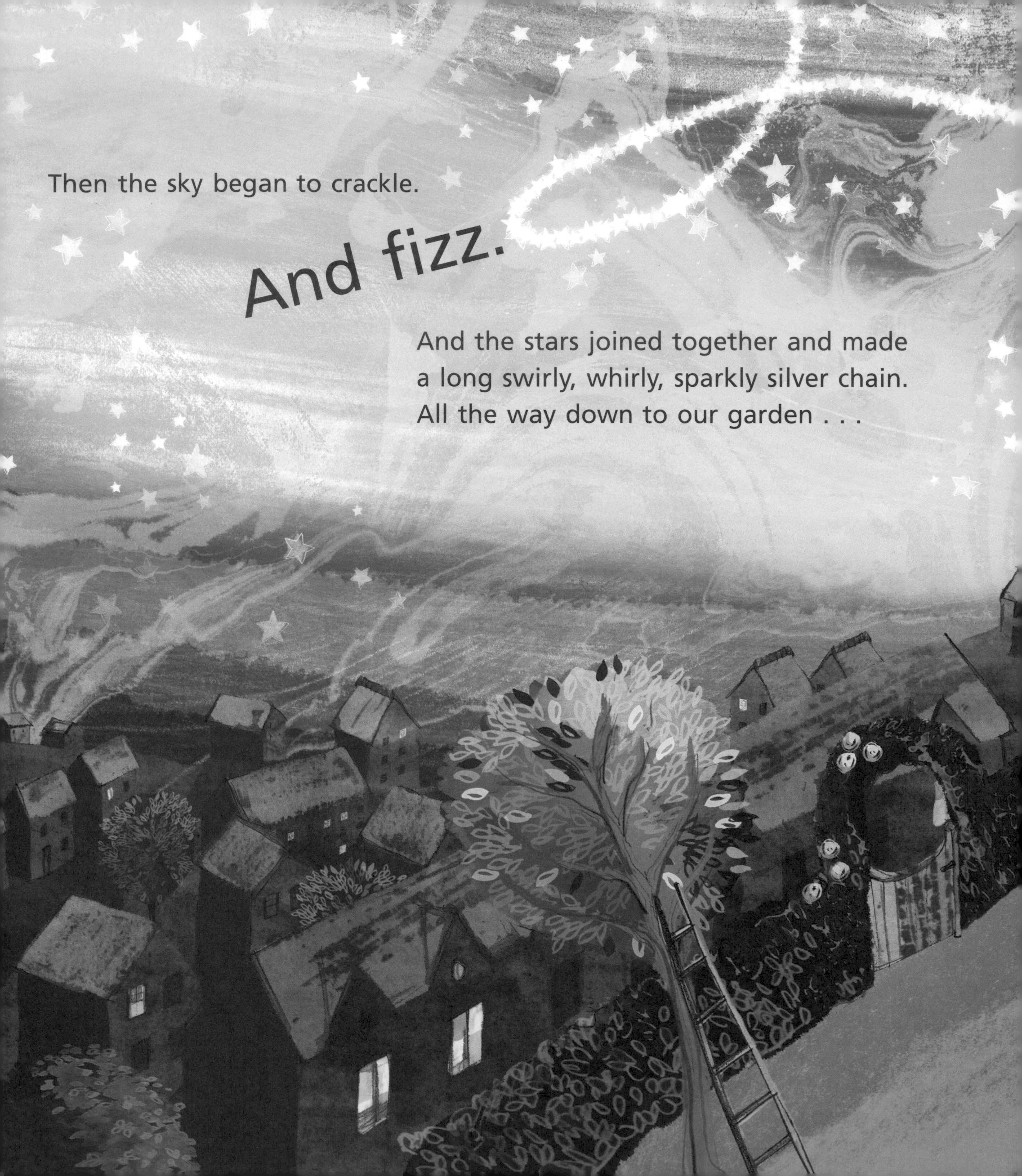